MW01598755

A Trail in the Forest

A Trail in the Forest

Marcus Robertson

Library of Congress Control Number: 2017908835
ISBN: Hardcover   978-1-5434-2747-9
                 Softcover   978-1-5434-2745-5
                 eBook   978-1-5434-2746-2

Print information available on the last page.

Rev. date: 07/22/2017

To order additional copies of this book, contact:
Xlibris
1-888-795-4274
www.Xlibris.com
Orders@Xlibris.com
762677

CONTENTS

My Friend 1

The Tree 3

Old Man Winter 7

The Wind 9

The Break 11

The Reason "Y" 15

The Clearing 17

The Aching 21

The Fog 25

The Dawn 31

Too Long 35

Dedicated to my exes

Every lesson I've learned from every mistake I've
made has made me stronger and wiser today.

My Friend

My friend loves me, this I know
For her smile tells me so
About my secret she cares not
As my rock she helps a lot

Fun and play at the beach all day
No fear I have to run away
Together as a team we fight
She sleeps at day and I at night

She leans on me and I on her
The road we travel is easier

The Tree

The air warms then cools; the winds change and begin
to pulse as they blow the leaves whither and thither.
"Come with me young man," the wind beckons.
Boom-boom, boom-boom. My heart races
and the wind picks up the pace.
Creak.
The limbs of a tree bend down to hug me;
it calms my heart and embraces me, shields
me, from the cold, blustering wind.
"Why do I love you?" I ask the tree. Such
as this was not meant to be!
The gardener did plant you here, and I am drawn
to your warm, strong branches. What would
the gardener think? Should I even care?
Tree, I do fear that we are banned and forbidden to play
in the field, the forest, and the garden. Where can we go?
I embrace the tree and hug it; my heart begins
to break. The love I feel cannot be.
Crash. The thousand pieces of my heart shatter
on the forest floor as the cold, biting wind
approaches me, but the tree and I are shielded!
But by whom?
The night has set – and though the wind does
blow – we are veiled in the shadows and masked
by night's darkness. But night only lasts so long.

Creak. The tree embraces me and I embrace it; I climb up its trunk and lie on its limbs feeling safe and secure, not wanting the moment to cease and knowing that the inevitable dawn approaches. Where will we go from here? When will the wind acknowledge us? When will it accept us?

I love you, tree.

Do you love me?

Old Man Winter

Winter whispers on the wind
"Hello boy," it says with a grin

Running, racing, unable to see
A killing coldness covers me

Jack Frost jumps and bites my nose
"Hurry, son, you haven't any clothes"

Nothing more naked in the forest than me
Trembling, troubling, weak in one knee

Faster, further, fighting to fly
Wasted winter will soon be nigh

The Wind

The wind is blowing once again. I must decide: do I
stand firm, or do I surrender to the wind and allow
it to throw me off the jagged cliff called emotion?
I ponder these things as I lie in bed, hot and bothered,
unable to decide. The window is open: opportunity
is there lurking behind the curtains that are now
tattered by the endless wind, the wind that is love.
My heart aches as the wind blows around my body.
Again, I ask myself: do I stand firm or do I surrender to
the wind and let it throw me off this emotional cliff?

The Break

I hate the wind and its wanton ways. I hate the
wind and the direction it pushes me in.
I loosen my grip on the tree.
"Why are you distant?" asks the tree.
"I thought you wanted me to explore?" I state.
"Ah yes," replies the tree, "you MUST
explore; I WANT you to explore."
I am frustrated to no end with him.
I do not want to leave, nor do I want to explore! I
wonder, 'does the tree not like me anymore?'
On the horizon I see a mirror, the mirror that reflects
my life, and I watch in curious wonder as it flies towards
me at unnatural speed, stopping just short of me, as I
now realize that I have climbed up over a hundred feet.
Briefly I see my reflection – and the tree behind
me – before the wind blows, and I watch in horror
as the mirror begins its disastrous descent.
The mirror has lost its footing and
now tumbles to its death.
As it falls it hits branches and begins to
crack. I feel my heart begin to break.
When it meets the ground below, it shatters
into confetti-sized sparkles. My heart is
broken; I want to cry but I cannot.
I want to scream and kick at the wind.
I have seen my fate, and the wind only pushes me harder.

My only choice is to fall; I don't want to fall!
I wonder, 'perhaps I can climb back down?'
But I know the tree would question my leaving,
and I would also have to contend with the force of
the wind; this would be painful and difficult.
Perhaps I could drop from branch to branch? But
what if I snap a branch and thus my leap becomes
a fall, becomes a self-fulfilling prophecy?
I recall the image that I first saw in the mirror: the
tree has missing branches, knobs that are still bloody.
I know the tree has been hurt by others like me.
I also recall seeing other figures in the tree.
The tree has told me about these other figures,
but can I trust the tree in all he says?
The tree has declared his love for me, but I am
still confused to his command: explore!
Perhaps one of the other shapes will provide the love the
tree needs, for it is apparent to me that I will not suffice.
It is time to move on.
I am frustrated and hurt by the tree, and yet in my
exploration I can think of nothing other than him.
I meet other trees: pecans, oaks, and pines.
But I do not embrace them nor feel the love
towards them that I felt with the tree.

The Reason "Y"

What am I?
Red

How am I?
Hot

Who am I?
Anger

Where am I?
Hell

When am I?
Too late

Why am I?
Really? You have to ask why? I'll tell you why
"Y" is a crooked letter that stands next to "Z"
"Y" is the accusation that's troubling me
"Y" is the reason I'm tangled in this mess
"Y" is the reason I feel distressed
Why, oh "Y", do you have to be
The crooked letter that troubles me?
You break all the rules and seem to run free

Perhaps that's why I'm so jealous of thee

The Clearing

I have made my way to the bottom of the gnarled tree
and have stepped conscientiously over the broken glass,
the bits of the mirror that once reflected my life. That
life is no more, I have chosen to chart a new course
and I am now strong enough to pursue it. I bear scars
on my arms, but the scars are reminders of the past;
I have to only touch them to know that they're real. I
now move forward and enter a clearing in the forest.
I hesitate to move forward into this clearing because
it is unfamiliar, but I see a rock that perhaps I can lie
on and rest from my weary descent. I am frightened
and utterly scared to move forward out into the open,
but deep down I find the strength to set my foot into
the sunlight. The sunlight feels warm and inviting;
it is so different from the shade of the forest.
"I'm curious about you," I say to the rock from afar.
"I'm curious about you, too," states the rock. I
begin to run; I want to embrace the rock!
"Stop!" yells the rock.
"You move too fast. I am neither an oak nor an
elm; I am made of stone. I am as old as the forest,
but I am considerably different. I do not bend
and sway as the trees do; I lie here and wait."
"I am hurt by your request to stop," I cry,
"but I do see you're different."

Now I am confused. The rock is interested in me, but yet it has asked me to stop. I turn with my head down and begin to return to the forest. Perhaps I am not as strong as I thought, but my name is called once again.
"Youngster! Why do you walk away?"
"You have asked me to stop. If I cannot move forward then I will find another way 'round."
"Youngster you misunderstand me!" the rock calls out.
'Did I truly misunderstand the rock?' I ask myself.
"How so?" I inquire.
"Move forward if you will, for I am indeed interested in you, but with me you must move slowly. Rocks are solid and heavy. Again, I neither bend nor sway."
So, after explaining my confusion to the rock I begin to move forward again, but this time at the pace the rock has requested: slowly. I am not running nor walking but crawling towards the rock.
"Please live here with me," the rock says.
"Here you can still play in the shade but also in the sun." I like this idea and welcome the invitation. I know that I have charted a new course, but I have not set any expectations other than I will rely upon the rock for support instead of the branches of trees.
"Tell me about yourself," I ask the rock.
"Then take a seat in the heather and we will exchange our stories," replies the rock.
I think I like the rock.

The Aching

I awaken!

The rock and the clearing were but a dream.
I have fallen from the treetops and now lie in the
shards of glass that were once the mirror of my life.

My dream of the rock turned quickly to nightmare.
The rock was not interested in me; he only used me.
Like a deer I walked into the clearing and was shot.
Assaulted.
Harassed.

Like the moonless night my heart is now void of any light.

There is another tree in the forest… I know him.
I do not want his kiss; I only want his embrace.
Even so, I really don't want to be touched anymore.

I hurt.
I ache.

I sit up.
I pull the bits of glass out of my face.
I pull the bits of glass out of my arm…
My leg…
My side.

The other tree, the tree I know, has left.
He was no help.
I alone am the one who pulled myself off the forest floor.

It's grown cold again.
I now feel comforted by the cold.
But, I am sad and afraid.

I hurt.
I ache.

I stand up and move away, but I don't make it far.

I collapse on the hard dirt of the forest floor.
The trees are so dense where I land
that the grass cannot grow.

I hurt.
I ache.

The cold dirt.
I sleep best in the cold.
I sleep again.

The Fog

When I wake, it is the middle of the night.
I am shocked to find that my hands have
become gnarled and my legs are twisted.
I am becoming a tree but yet this does not frighten me.
I am no longer a young boy who climbs
trees or dreams about rocks.
My skin is becoming tougher.
I feel a sense of exhilaration!
I am becoming a tree!
My roots begin to shiver as the cold sets
in. Fight or flight? I will fight!
I plunge my roots deeper into the soil and hang tight.
I stretch my branches to the North and South in
search of assistance, and I clutch onto the wise, strong
redwoods. Their roots are deep in wisdom, their
branches touch the heavens in divine reverence of the
stars, and their trunks are tough and steadfast. They
send the creatures of the forest for my protection.
I stand firm!
I am uneasy as the pumas climb my trunk; their claws
cause a sting but I am unharmed. The foxes surround my
roots, and I begin to feel warm again. I am tickled as the
snakes slither up my trunk, and then I feel my branches
bounce as squirrels jump on me, cheeks full of acorns.
The fog thickens and begins to rise; a wall of terrible
white is steadily rolling towards me. Demons' hands

begin to form in the mist; the foxes bare their teeth. Sinewy hands hurdle forward like gauntlets launched from cannons. The foxes snap and gnash their teeth. The fog rolls in and covers my roots; I cannot see, only hear their snarls and growls. The demons begin to grip my trunk and peel away the bark. I scream in pain, "I will not abide by your will. I am not yours to have; you do not own me! Leave now!" The coiled snakes unfurl like tightened springs, mouths gaping, fangs forward ready for the bite. "Why?!" cry out the demons. "We love you!"

Oh loathsome lovers, you only seek
to control me!" I scream.

"We will never stop, ever!" they shriek. "Come
home; we only want the best for you!"

"I AM HOME! Leave now!" I demand. The Redwoods tighten their grip and once again my roots dive deeper into the dark, rich soil and curl around rocks. I feel the safety of my fellow trees bracing me in support. More cold hands peel away my bark, and the fog surges upward to my branches where it is met by ferocious squirrels who pelt the hands with acorns and fan the fog away with their bushy tails. The pumas claw at the malevolent hands and rip the flesh to shreds.

"Leave my land and leave my grove! You
are not welcome here!" I cry.

"We go where we please; we control
the fog!" the demons laugh.

thump! thUMP! THUMP! The beating of wings grows closer and hawks land in my branches. Their claws hurt.

'Are they trying to lift me out of the ground? They haven't stopped flapping! What are they doing?' I wonder in fear. The wind produced by the hawks begins to dissipate the fog. I let go of the Redwoods and swing my branches forward. I pluck the hands off my trunk. "LEAVE ME BE!" I shout from the depths of my roots to the canopy of my branches. The demons retreat, but the fog remains I can see the foxes around my roots, and I see the blood dripping off their fangs. Others, less fortunate, lie maimed on the forest floor, lifeless; they fought hard for me. Using my roots, I open the forest floor and bury them while whispering quiet prayers of gratitude. I reach out again to the North and to the South to hug the Redwoods for sending me the strength of their creatures. I am now at peace.

The Dawn

The earth has reached its coldest point: the moment
just before the sun rises and darkness is still
covering the land in her shimmering cloak.
A single beam of light burns the early morning
fog and releases my mind from captivity.
I lift my root-legs and walk slowly because my feet
have become heavy. I can no longer run between
trees and out into clearings. I do not race across
the landscape like the young boy I once was.
I realize that I have been living in
a fog for many years now.
I have no idea where I'm going but only
that I am happy the sun is rising.
I know that I am searching for something
but I don't know what for.
I am more cautious now.
Now I am more aware of my surroundings; I am
more aware of the dangers that surround me. I am
aware of things that would gladly harm me.

Wet.
I stop.
I have walked into a river.
It is refreshing.

This is my new home.
I take root; I have become a tree.
Good-bye fog.
May the sun burn you into oblivion!

Too Long

My friend the robin has returned
To live in my branches undeterred
It's been so long
What can I say?
Not seen your face in 10,000 days
Take my branch and hold it tight
Wings around me, hug with all your might
Lines run deep now on your face
So many changes have taken place
Would you believe what I have seen?
I'm starting new, but I ain't green

CPSIA information can be obtained
at www.ICGtesting.com
Printed in the USA
LVOW08*1223290817
546714LV00005B/17/P